THE COLOUR OF

EXTINCTION

The Colour of
Extinction

S.C. FLYNN

RENARD PRESS

RENARD PRESS LTD

124 City Road
London EC1V 2NX
United Kingdom
info@renardpress.com
020 8050 2928

www.renardpress.com

The Colour of Extinction first published by Renard Press Ltd in 2024
For dates of first publication of individual poems, please see p. 64

Text © S.C. Flynn, 2024

Cover design by Will Dady

Printed and bound in the UK on carbon-balanced papers by CMP Books

ISBN: 978-1-80447-118-0

9 8 7 6 5 4 3 2 1

CONTENTS

The Colour of Extinction

PART ONE   3

  The Cruel Blank Edge

PART TWO   13

  Feathered Neurons

PART THREE   25

  Ancient Dust

PART FOUR   51

  Dry Gods Melting

THE COLOUR OF

EXTINCTION

To Claudia

PART ONE

the cruel blank edge

INHERITANCE

Under a sky the colour of extinction
you choose your own conclusion.
The earth might have already done so:
somewhere in its whirling mass of DNA
and infinite genetic possibilities
is the clue to what will replace us.
Perhaps an existing creature will evolve,
switching on latent capabilities
that have lain dormant for millennia,
or the distant descendants of extremophiles
currently clustered around hypothermal vents
and suspended from the roofs of caves
will develop in unimaginable ways.
But then again, maybe once is enough
and the world will embrace equality
with no striding master or dictator,
and ten thousand years of civilisation
will shrink to an unrepeated moment.

PANIC RESPONSE

Misled by unseasonal warmth,
a migrating bird returned too soon
shivers in the inexorable cold.
Each another world to conquer,
new islands in the Arctic
revealed by the melting ice.
Flowers alone in warm, bright fields,
waiting for bees that will never arrive.

THE TOMORROW SYNDROME

By the time we get there, it will be ours,
the future; no shocks, safe and familiar,
but there is so much to not think about,
and there will always be more from now on,
lurking just out of sight like hyenas
trailing us through each resource-war desert,
flooded shoreline and crowd of refugees,
every newly created slum or ruin,
waiting to crush the bones of resistance.

QUIET ANSWERS

There was once a language for Ireland's forests,
simple but unusual, like the life of plants,
without the glottal axe sounds we use today
to describe the empty hills that remain.
That language almost vanished with the trees,
marked for cutting along with the trunks,
and nearly lost in the crash of felling,
but now returns as vital oxygen.

FINAL CHAPTER

Start your story near the end and work backwards;
you don't know how much time is left to tell it,
so choose a point and begin – just begin –
maybe right before the cruel blank edge.
Very well: one foot was cut in two by the border,
toes floating in the unseen void,
every later step invisible.
The cracks alongside were eloquent;
thin alternate paths not followed
that closed for lack of traffic.
The trees by the road waved sign language,
warnings forever ignored.
I caught a glimpse of the past and future:
a concrete path where a chicken had walked
before it dried, leaving footprints
like writing on a large sheet of paper,
entering at top right and exiting,
after various twists, turns and pauses
to check out shiny nothings, at bottom left.
Start at the end because we are the end.

15,000 METRES

ABOVE TIME

In the eye of the cyclone
the most important event
has never taken place. Stillness
holds the world in a narcissistic trance:
silent greyness contemplating itself
under a dead star of spider dreams
in a galaxy you cannot escape.
You hold your breath without daring to whisper.
This eternity may be your last;
nature cannot die, so must suffer longest.

THE GREAT DYING

The predators are returning to the cities;
their gleaming eyes flit through rubbish dumps
and shine in the black depths of parks,
the only things really alive under the moon.
The golden lie still rings out,
but leafing through old books is no use now;
nor are the latest discoveries
of different ways of flying.
Death has climbed in through the open window
and the last of our fugitives
will soon be tracked and caught,
like tigers crushed by the coils of giant snakes.

ELEVEN KILOMETRES

Mariana Trench, Pacific Ocean

This is where life's journey ends –
the deepest well of the world's mind,
Mother Earth's vagina
and darkest subconscious.
The outside pressure would crush you flat;
remember what it's done to the creatures
we passed on the way, the world's deformed children
that it hides away for shame, floating nightmares
of tentacles and hard flattened bodies
that stay by their mother's side and do no harm.
But maybe you and I are the disgraces,
the ones who were born in the shallows above
and then crawled up on land and grew wild;
without the discipline of deepest water
our brains ballooned out, big and empty,
and now the clever wandering children
descend in technological incest.

PART TWO

feathered neurons

DINOSAURS ON THE ROOF

For the gulls of central Dublin

Some refugees have wings and live in our world
because we took theirs from them. The ancients
learnt much from birds, and so have I these years:
determination and adaptability,
fighting for what is important to you
and letting the world hear you state your case.
I will for ever remember them all:
Conor the Bold, foster-son and familiar;
Niamh the shrillest and Oisín the hoarsest;
Finbarr the Clown, who I've known from the egg;
Saoirse, wearing her leg ring like a model;
Lorcan the Explorer, who returns each spring.
Companions in the struggle of life,
sharing the great nest of our city.

COMMUTERS

The gulls arrive for work at dawn,
gliding in grey and white waves to their roofs
until every central building is covered
by the city's shrieking cerebral cortex
made of thousands of wings and ice-cold eyes,
acting as a single scaly-legged mind.
If a predator invades the colony,
a tornado of guards spontaneously forms
to drive off the danger with whirling attacks;
it is a kind of consciousness,
but all there is to see are countless moments
of flapping, screeching and raiding.
They all fly back to the coast in the evening,
driven by a single impulse,
feathered neurons in a vast limbic system,
sharing their dream of the sound of the sea.

AN EGYPTIAN VULTURE

IN DONEGAL

Searching for death and certain to find it,
this carrion drone is a guerrilla,
soaring on newly ignited thermals
in the brutal asymmetric warfare
between ourselves and the burning world,
a yellow-faced toolmaker dropping stones
on the rigid eggs of our complacency.
This ambassador carries its warning
to the ocean's edge on two-metre wings;
the mission might fail, but the message was sent.

CATHARSIS

The lesser black-backed gulls return each spring,
navigating from as far as Africa
by watching the sun and smelling the air,
risking predators, storms and exhaustion
to brighten the north with their laughing calls
and brilliant yellow legs, in a cycle
that has lasted for millions of years;
they cannot do otherwise, it seems.

No tempting illusion of free will
can take the blame for deaths on the way
or chicks carried off buildings by the wind;
for them it is the work of chance or fate,
to be lamented and suffered without regret
in the true spirit of tragedy.
Next year the beak-masked actors will be back
to present the festival once more.

EMERGENCE

Newgrange, County Meath

Just watch these starlings in the twilight,
thousands of them forming countless patterns,
ink swirling in this glass of evening.
Each bird's tiny impulses contribute
in magnifying freedom and beauty
to the very edge of limitless space;
the world's mind twisting and turning
right before our uncomprehending eyes,
hidden in mysterious symbols
deep as those on any ancient monument.

THE GATHERING

That clump of trees just up ahead
is pulsing and boiling with birds,
thousands packed tightly together like smoke;
a chattering, chirping autumn turbine
gathering energy for departure.
You can sense the power building, peaking
as more and more arrive, bending branches
under the weight of their massed impatience.
At a silent signal made every year
on this very day and at this hour
they all launch upwards in a giant ball
that twists and turns as fast as thought, stealing
so much life and instinct from this landscape
that will somehow make it through their absence;
you can see the hope and promise of spring
and the distant solemn march of winter
trail behind like rival festival flags
during their annual flutter in the wind.

HERON

Hunched inside her shabby cloak,
a lifeless tree with feathers and gleaming eyes
watching the unsuspecting world drift past,
a grey guardian of immobility;
prophecies from migrating or screeching birds
learn nothing from her stillness.
Then she strikes, unfolding a snaking neck
to stab with flashing beakspear,
shattering time's tranquil mirror
before retreating to her stasis.

HUNTERS OF THE LIGHT

The Arctic terns will soon be gone
to seek the endless daylight in Antarctica,
passing over Cretaceous cliffs of gulls
and then, while the sun grows hotter,
rivers of serotonin drained from cities;
diasporas of isolated minds
locked inside, dreading arrest in the night.
On they go, away from the darkness
that covers interrogation and famine,
above the fires and record temperatures
until they reach the melting ice of Dayworld.
When the days again get shorter they return,
craving the insomniac sun,
longing to sleep but fearing to dream.

EMPTY TREES

A town, complete in indifference,
where noon falls heavy as a concrete slab
and the days are long, bright and vast,
far too large for their meagre content,
waiting for the promised arrival of something.
There should be vultures on those branches
watching the efforts of the humans
to give a semblance of meaning to their lives,
but this silence slowly maturing
in a world bleached of meaning was their fate.
Wings of the past lightly brush your cheek,
and for a moment you see them again:
refugees migrating into extinction,
heads bowed against the bitter wind of time.

PART THREE

ancient dust

AFTER THE BUSHFIRE

The smouldering night has exhausted itself
and sunrise bleeds away the bruises,
slipping a red-gold mask over the landscape,
eyes half shut against the drifting ash.
Burnt trees stand in piles of cinders
that will soon be cold and dense as omens;
syllables of a scattered alphabet
asking questions of their ragged shadows.
Underneath the forest's puzzled face
and the ground's grey bankruptcy lie seeds
that have waited years for this, as if to say,
Let me breathe again, give me back the sky.

THE MEMORY OF WATER

Central Australia, 50,000 years ago

Every waterhole is smaller and further away
than the one before, and the plain no longer remembers
the forest that once stood here. They stagger on,
a clan of exhausted Diprotodon
seeking escape from the flooding dryness,
their mighty front claws scuffing up dust
that floats above in a choking cloud
and then settles on their fur,
mingling with the ash from the fires.
Ever more slowly they follow the memory of water,
where they will leave their massive bones to puzzled scientists
and the legend of the Bunyip to the Dreamtime.

ONE DARKNESS HOLDS

THEM ALL

Stingrays are the underwater shadows
of the distant beaches of my childhood:
gliding abysses with dead eyes and clown mouths
below the clear surface and slow gleaming days,
passing back and forth all summer long
and constantly prowling the sand of my dreams.
Species are currents in an ocean of genes –
adapting, evolving, disappearing –
and the interlocking puzzle of my self
has changed since then in ways I cannot see,
but the black shapes of the stingrays still coast
in unchanging, restless eternity.

LAST SYMPHONY

When the man first sat in this armchair
the house was full of wife and children,
but they all went away as usual
and quiet has taken their place,
so that his slowing footsteps echo
and fading shadows of things already known
surface and sink in his mind. So now
he sits and hears much more than ever.
The world outside has never stopped playing:
bird song, buzz of insects, wind and rain,
possums skittering above the ceiling,
the scrape of leaves and branches on the roof.
Before too long, the chair will be empty,
but the concert will go on and on.

PHASE CHANGE

Somehow I always know when it starts;
when the locusts have reached the point of swarming
and the desert breaks away to fly all night,
desperately seeking the green it cannot see,
a book of a billion fluttering pages
carried on the wind, each square metre teeming
with thousands of voracious lives. I wait,
sweating in bed while the cloud rolls on,
until the advance guard rains on the roof.
Tomorrow the streets will be littered
with dry, rattling dead swept by the breeze
and a few solitary, calm survivors,
while I will be pale and exhausted,
waiting for the cycle to begin once more.

HOPE

Leeuwin Lighthouse, Western Australia

The Indian and Southern oceans touch
and then follow separate destinies.
Humpback whales roll in the water, slapping
their fins to send out spray and messages.
Seabirds carry nest materials, dropping
little pieces on the way as signposts.
A magpie lands close by and sings – maybe
to my red jumper, maybe to the future.

THE SHEARING SHED

Boiling and roaring by day,
the shearing shed traps heat, noise and sweat
while thousands of sheep pass through, sliding
on floors and ramps to leave their wool
to the snarling machines and barking dogs.
At night in the blissful cool
the shed releases it all and goes quiet,
except for the splash of a possum or fox
that falls in the water tank,
where it circles and circles,
unable to climb out.

HORIZON DREAMING

Streams of flying ants are bursting
from the ground, pouring out
through cracks in the hard baked dirt
like jets of steam from a heaving cake;
not thrown into this world to find their way
but bridging earth and sky
for a million simultaneous moments
on fresh disposable wings,
thrust up by an annual depth impulse
that millions of years still haven't satisfied
and then whirring into the blue furnace
towards a future as ancient
as the endless red dust they come from.

TREE GODS WEEPING

Karri forest, Western Australia

The rain has left its offering;
eucalyptic freshness floods the cool, damp air
and leaves drip deities' tears
on the little humans far below,
who crane their necks and squint
to see the waving tops caress the sky.
These gods are never cruel,
but distant and indifferent
like others of their kind. The rain returns.

THE EXILE

Meteorite in the Australian desert

Nothing here has changed at all
since this burnt rock thrust itself
deep in dirt red as sword wounds
all those millions of years ago.
Once the noise that no one heard had faded
and the cloud of blood that hid the sky
had settled, this exile waited
for someone or something that might evolve
while the constellations slowly swirled
around an unseen vortex:
teardrops of angels
stirred into a black cup of loneliness
by the finger of a hand so vast
that even the gods of the galaxies
would not know what to call it.

Our planet scorched a hundred mouths
on this ragged surface,
but they all speak unknown languages;
maybe those to be will learn them all
and come to understand
that not everything has a reason.

There should be many others
gathered round this patient grail
to watch until that day arrives,
but there's only me sitting in the dust
among the countless shrubs
and ants glinting in the sun.
As the sprawling wash of black
sweeps the desert cold,
I warm my hands over this stone
that lost its heat
before there was anyone to feel it;
I'm made from the same stellar slag heap,
equally cold and ancient
and just as alone and uncomprehended.

SALT LAKE

Sometimes the future's flight is straight and smooth
like shining summer runways,
but then it brings you way out here
where the ground is endless crust
that snaps underneath your feet
to free the thick black sludge that lurks below
and where the trees are pale dry prisoners
thrust deep in permanent winter,
their bony arms stretched wide in pleading
to whoever might have put them here.
Perhaps they come alive each night and clash –
giant skeletons under polished moon shield –
sharp cracking blows breaking a silence
that no one has ever heard,
but then as dawn approaches they stiffen,
joints crunching as their backs grow rigid
and their hands lift once again in agony
as they stand to face the sun's cruel gaze
like driftwood carved with strange inscriptions.

This is my for-ever world. I walk in,
crunching through the flat white sheet
to sink in the squelching dark below
so my footsteps stretch behind me
like black ink spattered on a page;

no wind will ever shift them,
so when one day you reach this place
you'll know just what they mean.
I belong out here where nothing changes;
soon I'll be just a dense heart of decay,
an elemental core of toxic life waste,
my attention span shrunk to a painful dot
while random dreams circle round my head.
I take my place among the guilty naked;
my roots were poisoned long ago
and now my limbs can harden and set.

THE CONTINENT OF INSECTS

Australia is really theirs:
for hundreds of millions of years
they have fought each other
and the brutal landscape
in primordial arms races
that developed specialised workers,
warriors with pincers and shielding
and sophisticated social structures.
Wars and alliances between them
still come and go, like their cities,
while elsewhere humans in parallel
are living out their noisy moment.

GHOST TOWN

Gold rush memory in the desert
half-buried in the scorching sand,
mummified by the dry heat
as if it were alive last year.
Mounds of earth sprawl to the horizon,
traces of thousands of digging dreams.
Looking through the door,
you can see the ruins of civilisation;
filtered through a sieve, the earth leaves tiny shells,
remnants of an inland sea.

WALKABOUT

Termite mounds, northern Australia

Termite Mounds at Dawn

Silence is cruel, they always say,
but so is constant talk. If you were here,
you'd taste these endless cones of stillness
and smell their patience melting on your hands;
these sundials throw shadows but time is sleeping.
You would like to hear me say I miss you,
but there's nothing I lack out here
except the secret of the mounds.

An Opened Mound

I shove a crooked stick in the crust
of the driest-looking mound,
stirring ancient dust that stings my eyes;
no dead thing rises from this tomb.
Instead life itself comes pouring out,
cool and damp in tiny white packets,
guarding its treasure with pincers and riddles –
life that is older than dinosaurs
but will still be new when we are gone.

III
Dreaming the Mounds

As the sun went down and the moon came out
I sat, thirsty and hot, among the towers;
they turned my heat into freshness
and the dry baked air into moisture.
These are blocks of pure life, not gravestones,
some older than love, some newer than peace;
magnetic cathedrals of spark and dust
that hoard no creeping death in their crypts.
They grow again from the bones of spirits,
phallic towers of the earthly mother
eroded by wind but never shrunk,
battering rams that break down eras.
There's a pattern in their order;
they launch the code to our satellites
and to stars that are gone or yet to be.

The Mounds Speak

I scramble up the highest tower
like a war priest climbing a pile of heads,
clinging on somehow among the rubble
as sheets of sand and dust slide down the sides
and ants swarm thick around my feet.
I spread my arms out, stretching north and south
to make a sunburnt aerial. The mounds
are in my mind and I am their voice;
the loudest of all in the land of the deaf.

THE OXYGEN MAKERS

Stromatolites in Shark Bay, Western Australia

I
Midday, Water's Edge

Don't take breathing for granted;
it hasn't always been so easy.
The fresh twenty-one per cent we live on
was made by these slimy cyan domes
over billions of silent years, puff by puff.
Somewhere we've failed, made it all go wrong;
but these patient workers could do it all again.

II

Late Afternoon, Ankle Deep

I throw my phone in the warm shallow water;
I could never tell you what it is I see.
I throw in my watch; counting seconds is pointless
where nothing has changed since before there were fish.
I throw in my keys; the iron they are made of
was oxidised by these round turbines
while the air was still rank from creation.
I throw in my sunglasses; without these domes
there never would have been an ozone layer.

III

Early Evening, Knee Deep

I'm not afraid to go further out
into the maternal warmth of the water
that wraps my legs like a birth blanket;
the plesiosaurs stay far away
from these extra salty shallows.
A pterodactyl kite shadow flits
across my shoulder, flying on
to better hunting. I breathe deep;
the air is richer than you'll ever know –
our twenty-one per cent tastes more like thirty
in the dense Cretaceous heat.

Sunset, Floating Face Down

I am as old and as young as the domes;
there is still so much to do to change the world.
My back soaks up the late Precambrian sun
just as they do, but there is so little life
in the air, so little; all we need is time.

PART FOUR

dry gods melting

ANTARCTIC VOICES

Sometimes when the wind here talks
it tells me things that science will never say:
how long ago by different stars
the gods of night and day agreed
to split the year between them;
that jutting rocks above the snow
are the eggs of enormous stone birds
and every iceberg is a wayward child
running away from home;
how the sky god bled the world of colour
to make the southern lights;
that rolling balls of snow
are tossed around by baby giants
while their parents' snores from underground
pile up stacks of frozen steam
and that the penguins march away each year
to seek the trick of flight;
and how much more the cold would tell me
if I could catch its icy tongue.

ANTARCTIC YELLOW

You've come all this way for the Southern Lights,
but they're on strike again. Then someone says,
Let's go see the snow petrel,
the cute white dove that bathes in the snow
of the continent of peace,
and on the way you wonder
if you could belong like the petrel.
But it's far to these rocks
and you learn what cold can mean,
so you ask yourself
if you really need to see Antarctica
or just to know that it's down here somewhere.
Then this bird that's guarding its chick
spits hot yellow stuff in your face.
It stinks of fish and won't come off
and you'll wear this colour and smell
like an oily tattoo;
now you can say you belong.

OXYGEN DICTATORSHIP

One eye watching the emptiness all around
and the faded sketch of hostility above,
sleeping whales are boundary markers
suspended vertically just below the surface,
cordoning off a hemispheric dream space:
half of each gigantic brain awake
while the other dives deep in the subconscious,
pursuing unimaginable prey
hidden in the limitless expanse,
until the need to breathe calls them back once again.

VOYAGE OF THE ICEBERG

Shipwrecked Iceberg Breaking Free

A penguin sneezes and the world erupts.
That grinding groan you hear
is the sound of a continent making love,
the blue mountain heaving and churning
under the flat white sheet.
Do you still think that if we weren't here to listen
the sound would cease to be,
or have you understood at last
how small we are, how brief?
The things that used to mean so much
on our boiling bridge of words
count less than a seal's snorts in a hole.

Plausibly Blue

Under the frozen anaemia of summer,
the still air smells like dry gods melting.
The iceberg hides its whiteness in this blue,
hoarding the red light like dragons' jewels
and letting go the violet rays;
if it could hold those fast as well,
the mountain would drift by like a black hole,
sucking in the light and giving nothing back
except a passing touch of phantom cold
and a gentle fizz as it spits out
ancient air that dinosaurs might have breathed.
This giant piece of mosaic
has dripped up the cloudy glass
at the bottom of the world,
snatching fossils and mummified lichen
and bringing ages of close-packed memories;
permafrost answers to a world of questions
that will soon melt away, but not just yet.
There's still time to feel the quiet ghosts
writhing under our boots
if we softly rush without slipping.

III
Boarding the Iceberg

I follow a bunch of chattering penguins
to the rending scrape of the widening gap
and then jump off the continent.
The iceberg wrenches free at last
and the penguin crew waddle above
to raise our flag of peace.
We have screeching skuas as lookouts
and whales and seals as escorts,
so we set off to find Australia;
it's somewhere over there
and twenty million years ago.

IV
Voyage of the Iceberg

Now evening's wearing midday's face.
Our floating time capsule, still sparkling and popping,
is shoving through the flimsy sea ice.
I now feel Gondwanan voices
simmering beneath my feet;
every rising bubble of air
that gouges our tall ship's sides
carries off a puff of history.
The penguins dive one by one in the water,
hunting the fish that hunt the krill
that hunt the microbes around the iceberg.
This chain of life trails on behind
our slowly shrinking country
that drifts away from treaties
and out of reach of governments
towards a dissolving future.

V

Abandoning the Iceberg

And can you tell me what it's all about,
this endless jumping on and off the world?
The skuas, whales and seals have all turned back
and the penguins found refuge on an ice floe.
This is how a species dies out,
when all the rest abandon ship,
while the slow or stubborn stay on board,
fading away in slow fatigue.
A while ago I felt the cold,
but now I don't feel much of anything.

VI
The Passenger

Then in a patch of clearer ice I see him:
a bearded man with an outstretched hand.
I want to dig him out and ask him who he was,
but then he's gone and the ice is milky.
Still, we've got months to go until the night,
and by then the ice man will have melted free.
We'll have no stars to steer by
except the tireless sensors in the satellites
that track our gobbled microwaves,
out here where only the sky has eyes.
Can you see me up there? I'm waving.

ACKNOWLEDGEMENTS

Thanks to: Claudia, who always believed; my parents, who inspired my love of nature; Will Dady, who understood and appreciated; and Sir David Attenborough, for many years of wonderful programmes that fired my imagination.

DATES OF FIRST PUBLICATION

'Inheritance' first published in *The Honest Ulsterman*
'Panic Response' first published in *A Thin Slice of Anxiety*
'The Tomorrow Syndrome' first published in *Gaia Lit*
'Quiet Answers' first published in *Seventh Quarry*
'Final Chapter' first published in *Unapologetic*
'15,000 Metres above Time' first published in *Ecozona*
'The Great Dying' first published in *D.O.R.*
'Eleven Kilometres' first published in *Anvil Tongue*
'Dinosaurs on the Roof' first published in *Orbis*
'Commuters' first published in *New Critique*
'An Egyptian Vulture in Donegal' first published in *D.O.R.*
'Catharsis' first published in *Urban*
'Emergence' first published in *Ragaire*
'The Gathering' first published in *The Roscommon Herald*
'Heron' first published in *Causeway*
'Hunters of the Light' first published in *Anvil Tongue*
'Empty Trees' first published in *The Ecological Citizen*
'After the Bushfire' first published in *Gaia Lit*
'The Memory of Water' first published in *Gaia Lit*
'One Darkness Holds Them All' first published in *Cyphers*
'Last Symphony' first published in *Orbis*
'Phase Change' first published in *Osmosis*
'Hope' first published in *Fearless* anthology
'The Shearing Shed' first published in *Prole*
'Horizon Dreaming' first published in *ZiN Daily*

'The Exile' first published in *The Orphic Review*

'Salt Lake' first published in *Fevers of the Mind*

'The Continent of Insects' first published in *The Galway Review*

'Ghost Town' first published in *Lothlorien*

'Walkabout' I first published in *Dreich*; III and IV first published in *A Thin Slice of Anxiety*

'The Oxygen Makers' first published in *D.O.R.*

'Antarctic Voices' first published in *The Ecological Citizen*

'Antarctic Yellow' first published in *The Galway Review*

'Oxygen Dictatorship' first published in *Synchronised Chaos*

'Voyage of the Iceberg' I first published in *Cyphers*; II first published in *Antipodes*; III first published in *Ecozona*; IV and V first published in *Tír na nÓg*; VI first published in *A New Ulster*

A NOTE ON SUSTAINABILITY

RENARD PRESS feels strongly that there is no denying the climate crisis, and we all have a part to play in fixing the problem.

We are proud to be one of the UK's first climate-positive publishers, taking more carbon out of the air than we put in. How? We reduce our emissions as much as possible, using green energy, printing locally and choosing the materials we use carefully; we calculate our carbon footprint and doubly offset it through gold-standard schemes; and we plant a tree for every order we receive via our website to give back to the planet.

Find out more at:

RENARDPRESS.COM/ECO